The Pea Blossom

Retold and illustrated by Amy Lowry Poole

Holiday House / New York

3 5 7 9 10 8 6 4 2

Library of Congress Cataloging-in-Publication Data

Poole, Amy Lowry.
The pea blossom / retold by Amy Lowry Poole. —1st ed.
p. cm.

Based on the Hans Christian Andersen story: Five peas in a pod.

Summary: In a garden near Beijing, five peas in a shell grow and wait to discover what fate has in store for them.

ISBN 0-8234-1864-2 (hardcover)
ISBN 0-8234-2018-3 (paperback)

[1. Fairy tales. 2. Peas—Fiction. 3. China—Fiction.]
I. Andersen, H. C. (Hans Christian), 1805–1875. Fem fra en ærtebælg.
II. Title.

PZ8.P795Pe 2005
[E]—dc22   2003067544

ISBN-13: 978-0-8234-1864-0 (hardcover)   ISBN-10: 0-8234-1864-2 (hardcover)
ISBN-13: 978-0-8234-2018-6 (paperback)   ISBN-10: 0-8234-2018-3 (paperback)

To my mother,
Barbara Schueler Lowry,
from the fifth pea

Once upon a time, in a small garden near the great city of Beijing, there were five peas in one shell. They were green, and they believed that the whole world must be green, for that was all that they knew.

The summer sun shone down on the tiny peas nestled in their shell, and the peas began to grow. Summer rains came and moistened the peas, and they grew even larger. Their shell soon became tight and uncomfortable.

"Are we going to sit here forever?" asked the first pea. "There must be something outside. Something bigger and better than this. I can feel it.

"I'm going to get out of here and fly up to the sun," he boasted. "I'll dance with the raven who rules the day."

The second pea spoke up. "I'll do better than that," he declared. "I'm going to fly to the moon and dance with the toad who rules the night."

The third and fourth peas decided that they were going to fly to the palace and dine with the emperor.

"And what will you do?" they asked the fifth and smallest pea.

The little pea thought for a moment and replied, "I shall go wherever it is that I am meant to."

Time passed and the shell began to turn yellow.
The peas began to fidget. They were impatient—
all except the fifth pea, who was content to wait.

Suddenly they felt a pull on the shell. It was torn open,
and the peas tumbled into the hand of a boy. In his other
hand the boy held a hollow reed. He looked down at the peas
and said, "These are the perfect peas for my peashooter."

And with that he grabbed the first pea and shot him
high into the air.

"I'm going to the sun at last!" exclaimed the first pea.

The pea landed in a gutter and was eaten by a pigeon.

The boy picked up the second pea and launched him toward the garden. He landed in a dark well.

"My, how dark the moon is," said the second pea, and soon sank to the bottom of the well, where he was swallowed by a frog.

The third and fourth peas got their wishes, for they landed in a rice bowl and were served to the emperor for dinner.

The fifth pea trembled as the boy rolled him into the peashooter. "What is to happen will happen," he said, and sighed.

With that he flew up into the sky and bounced onto a windowsill of a tiny house. He rolled into a crevice lined with leaves and soft moss, and lay still. "What is to happen will happen," he repeated to himself.

Within the house lived a poor woman who went out to clean stoves and chop wood for the townspeople of Beijing. She worked hard, for she had a daughter who was frail and weak and lay day after day in her bed. The daughter had been sick for a whole year, and it seemed as if she could neither live nor die.

Soon winter came. The pea was cold and fell asleep under his cover of moss and leaves. The mother struggled to care for her daughter, but the girl got weaker and weaker. The woman feared that her daughter would soon die and moved her bed away from the window.

After many cold months, spring arrived at last, and the sun began to shine again through the little window. The girl raised her head weakly and looked outside. There she spied the green tendrils of a pea plant moving gently in the wind. She called to her mother, who came and opened the window.

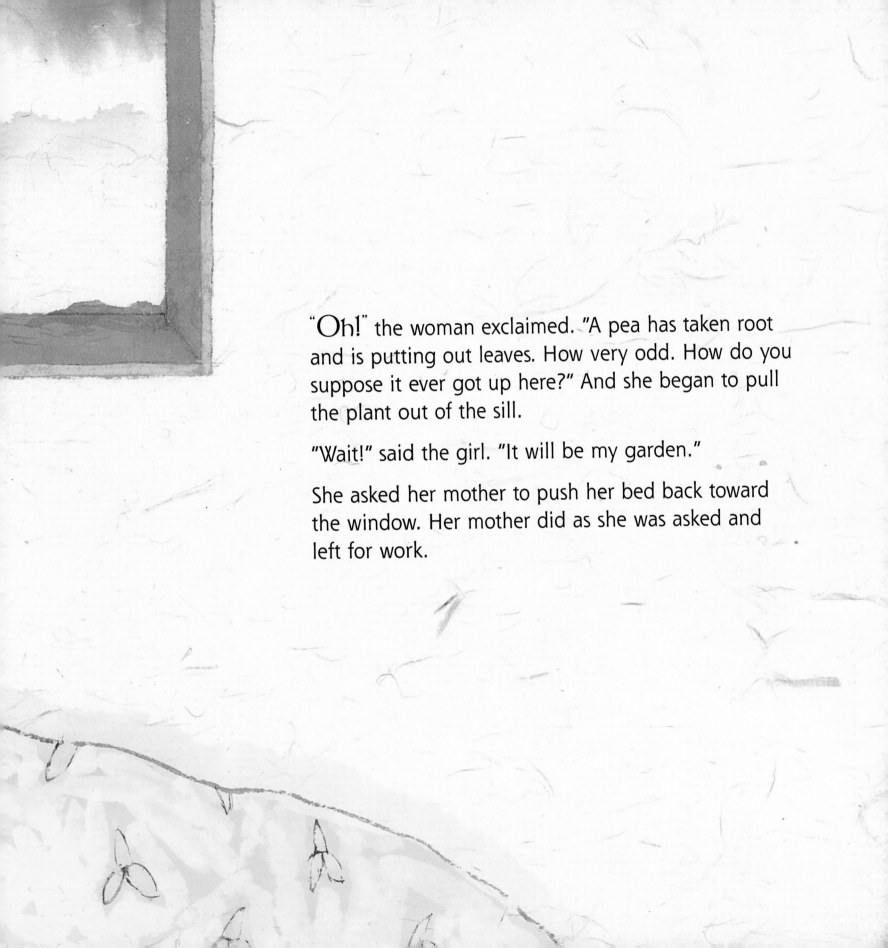

"Oh!" the woman exclaimed. "A pea has taken root and is putting out leaves. How very odd. How do you suppose it ever got up here?" And she began to pull the plant out of the sill.

"Wait!" said the girl. "It will be my garden."

She asked her mother to push her bed back toward the window. Her mother did as she was asked and left for work.

The girl looked out and watched the little pea plant dance in the wind. When her mother came home, they fashioned a support for the pea with a stick and some string, so that it might not be broken by the winds. The little plant began to grow and soon wrapped its tendrils around the windowsill. The girl was entranced and the color began to return to her cheeks.

After a month the girl was able to sit up. The little plant began to blossom, and soon the windowsill was covered with tiny blue flowers.

Pods sprouted from the blossoms, and small peas formed within smooth green shells. And as the peas grew fat in their pods, so did the girl thrive and become healthy again.

The fifth and smallest pea was now a vine of green leaves and pods. "This is what was meant to happen," he said, and smiled to himself, happy and content.

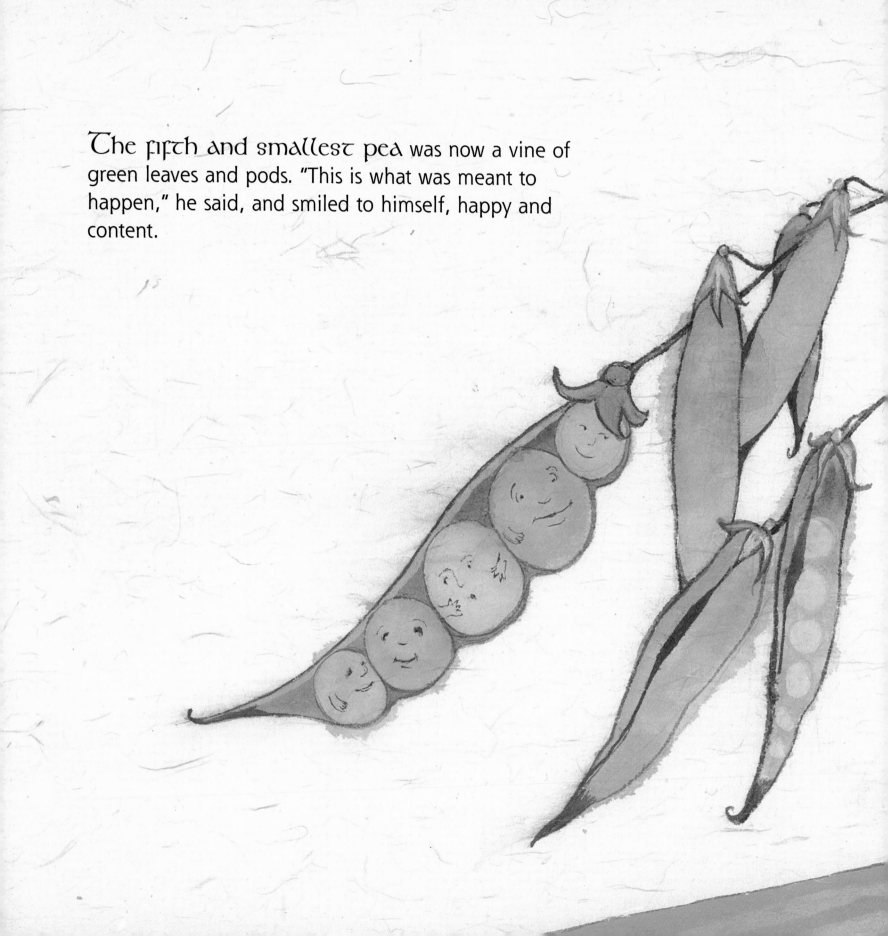

Author's note

Hans Christian Andersen was born on April 2, 1805, in a small village in Denmark. Two hundred years later, his fairy tales and stories are still read and loved by people all over the world.

Born into a humble family, Andersen did not attend much school. However, his lack of education did not stop him from pursuing his dreams. When he was fourteen years old, Andersen moved to Copenhagen, where he worked in the theater as an actor, singer, and dancer. A director at the Royale Theatre read one of Andersen's plays and helped the teenager return to school. After completing grammar school and studying at the University of Copenhagen, Andersen began a successful career as an author of plays, novels, travel literature, and, of course, his famous fairy tales and stories.

I read "The Pea Blossom" as a child, and loved the idea that something as small and simple as the pea plant could help nourish a sick child and bring her back to health. I admired

the fifth and smallest pea because, unlike the others, he was content to accept his fate, which eventually led him to a fulfilling new life. The pea's gentle nature reminded me of people I have admired, including some of the artists I had worked alongside in China. The tale of the pea's patience and caring have, I think, a universal appeal that speaks to people of all cultures. I was thus inspired to retell the story and set it in Beijing.

My interest in China grew out of my experiences living in Beijing in the 1990s. At that time much of the city was surrounded by *hutongs*, or alleys and lanes, that led to small gates and low houses. These were often arranged in quadrangles, which are building complexes located around a four-sided courtyard. Oftentimes the residents of these homes were poor, especially those on the outskirts of the city, and many kept simple vegetable gardens.

The first two peas in the pod refer to the raven in the sun and the toad in the moon. According to ancient Chinese mythology, a three-legged raven inhabits the sun. The raven's three legs denote the three phases of the sun: dawn, midday, and dusk. In contrast to this symbol is a frog or toad that rules the damp night and lives on the moon.